DETECTIVE DUCK

DUCK

BOOK 1

Cataloging-in-Publication Data has been applied for and may be obtained from the Library of Congress.

ISBN 978-1-4197-5513-2

Text © 2023 Henry Winkler and Lin Oliver
Illustrations © 2023 Dan Santat
Book design by Deena Micah Fleming

Printed and bound in China
10 9 8 7 6 5 4 3 2 1

Amulet Books are available at special discounts when purchased in quantity for premiums and promotions as well as fundraising or educational use. Special editions can also be created to specification. For details, contact specialsales@abramsbooks.com or the address below.

ABRAMS The Art of Books
195 Broadway, New York, NY 10007
abramsbooks.com

Frances Joan . . . Your dreams are
never too big . . . You are so powerful.
—Papa

For my beloved granddaughter, Noa Baker,
and her beloved mom, Julia Stein.
—L.O.

For Leah, Alek, and Kyle.
—D.S.

CHAPTER I

Willow Feathers was the only duck in the world whose father was a beaver. Most ducks are raised by ducks, just like most snails are raised by snails and most giraffes are raised by giraffes. But not Willow. Her father was Beaver McBeaver, and the two of them lived in a dam he had built on Dogwood Pond.

When she was just an egg, a strong wind blew Willow from her mother's nest. Day after day, the egg floated downstream until it got snagged in the sticks of Beaver McBeaver's dam. There, Willow hatched and grew into a fluffy duckling, with a yellow bill as bright as a raincoat.

Beaver McBeaver named her Willow after his favorite tree, and Feathers because, unlike him, she was covered in them.

Willow loved to spend her days poking under every blade of grass and rock at Dogwood Pond.

"My, my, you sure are curious," Beaver McBeaver said to her one day as he watched her exploring the pond.

"I want to be a detective when I grow up," she told him. "And solve mysteries. Lots and lots of mysteries."

"A detective!" her father exclaimed, smiling broadly and showing off his long front teeth. "That's a big dream for a little duck!"

That made Willow feel sad, because it made her feel small. And nobody wants to feel small.

Her father noticed. He was a very good father and didn't want his daughter to be sad.

"On the other hand, it's good to have a goal," he added quickly. "And if you really want to become a duck detective, your curiosity will come in very handy. It can lead you to great adventures."

Just hearing the word *adventure* gave Willow hope. It made her heart race with excitement. She loved to explore. She loved to collect hidden treasures. And most of all, she loved to use her smart duck brain to solve problems.

As the sun rose high in the sky, Beaver McBeaver went off to collect more sticks for his dam. A beaver's work was never done. Willow fluffed her feathers and waddled off to find an adventure. She started with her best friend, Sal.

"I'm looking for a mystery to solve," she said to him.

"You're just like Detective Detect-O," Sal told her, shooting out his tongue to catch a fly. He missed, as usual.

Sal was a black salamander with yellow spots who loved to read comic books. He was a better reader than a hunter. Every morning, he would

lie under a pile of damp leaves and read scraps of comic books that children had left behind at the nearby campground. When the scraps got too soggy to read, he didn't mind. He used them as washcloths. He liked to keep his yellow-spotted face mud-free.

"Oh, I wish I could be a real detective," Willow said. "But I'm just a little duck. I could never be as brave or as smart as Detective Detect-O."

"You can do anything you want," Sal told her, pointing one toe right at her face. "Look at me: I'm a salamander and I can read. Show me another salamander who can do that!"

Willow nodded, but deep down, she didn't really believe Sal. *It's easy to say you can do whatever you want*, she thought, *but it's hard to actually do it.*

A mosquito swooped down from the trees and buzzed right by them.

"Oh, there's my lunch," Sal said. "Gotta go."

He scurried after the mosquito and disappeared into the ferns. Willow went over to her secret hiding place, a shady spot hidden in the reeds. She took out her Stuff Box, which she kept hidden behind a moss-covered rock.

Sitting down on the bank of the pond, she sorted all the stuff she kept in her Stuff Box.

"Oh look, here's the red ribbon I found hanging on the dogwood tree," she said. She took the ribbon from the box and made herself a little ponytail.

"And here's that spoon I found in the waterfall. If humans had a bill like mine, they wouldn't have to scoop up their food with this silly thing."

Suddenly, Willow heard a rustling in the plants behind her. She turned around and saw the tip of a long black tail poking out from the patch of green ferns. She knew who that tail belonged to: It was Snout, the weasel.

Snout lived in the nearby woods, and he was a sneaky, tricky, mean, no-good thief. He was always looking for a chance to pounce on Willow and steal something from her Stuff Box.

Willow searched her box and grabbed a rubber band she had found. Putting one end in her bill and the other end around her webbed foot, she aimed the rubber band right at Snout's tail . . . and then let it fly!

It shot through the air like a rocket.

Zoom! Whoosh! Snap!

"Ow!" yelped Snout.

"There's more where that came from, you thief!" Willow shouted. She made her voice sound brave, but underneath, she felt as shaky as a feather in a windstorm.

"I'll be back, you silly duck!" he yelled as he tucked his tail between his legs and ran.

Just then, Willow heard a noise. It was loud and booming like thunder or a giant tree falling.

Thumpity, thumpity, crash, boom, bang!

That noise was much louder than anything an angry weasel could make!

Willow was so frightened, she couldn't even quack. She turned her head and saw a huge black object rolling toward the pond.

And it was heading right toward her.

CHAPTER 2

Willow dove behind a pine tree just in time and covered her head with her wings. Peeking out, she saw the large black object crash into the pond. It created a wave so high, the water flooded the banks and almost washed her away. She jumped into her Stuff Box to hold it down and sputtered to catch her breath.

"Sal!" she managed to call out. "Help!"

"Is it Snout?" he replied from the reeds. "Tell him to keep his stinky weasel paws off your things. We're tired of him sneaking around our pond."

"It's not Snout!" Willow cried. "It's worse than that. Come quick!"

Sal scurried to Willow's side.

"Look!" she said, pointing to the huge black object that was now bobbing up and down in the pond. "What in the world is that?"

Sal knew immediately what it was.

"It's an alien spaceship," he said. "We've been invaded!"

"Are you sure?"

Sal rushed to his pile of leaves and returned with the comic book he was reading.

"Look," he squeaked, pointing to the cover. "The thing in our pond looks just like this. It's a spaceship from Jupiter. It's probably filled with one-eyed aliens!"

"Oh no! Do you think they're going to eat us?"

"Probably," a deep voice said. It was Harry, the catfish who lived at the bottom of Dogwood Pond. Harry was never in a good mood but was especially unhappy right now. "Their spaceship could have crushed us," he said. "And not one of them has come out to apologize."

"That's true." Willow nodded. "These aliens have very bad manners."

"And there could be thousands of them just waiting to attack us," Sal said with a gasp.

"Wait. You're flying off the handle without any proof," Willow said to Sal. "Let's call Flitter and send her out to investigate. That's what a real detective would do."

Willow let out a long, low honk. It was the danger call. Across the pond, Flitter was sunning herself on a whip-poor-will with some of her dragonfly pals. When she heard the call, she zipped through the air to Willow.

"We're being invaded," Sal told Flitter, twitching his skinny tail back and forth.

"Very rude aliens from Jupiter," added Harry, "who want to eat us for lunch."

"Who'd want to eat me?" Flitter said. "I'm so little, I wouldn't even fill up a fish's smelly belly."

"My belly is not smelly," Harry grumbled. "My breath might be, but it's part of my charm."

"Flitter," Willow said, "we need you to learn more about these aliens. Find out where their spaceship came from. Can you do that?"

"Of course," Flitter answered. "I'm a dragonfly. I was born to fight dragons."

"Um . . . here's the thing, Flitter," Sal said. "They aren't dragons, they're aliens."

"No problem," Flitter said. "I can handle them with my two left wings tied behind my back."

Flitter took off into the air. She glided above the pond, doing flips and circles over the treetops and meadows, until she spotted the nearby dirt road. Through the dust and the morning mist, she caught sight of the problem.

It was large and red and looked like a metal, fire-breathing dragon.

CHAPTER 3

Flitter flew lower to get a better look. She noticed something moving next to the red dragon.

I know what that is, she thought. *It's a human. One of those big hairy creatures who wear funny-looking clothes and lace-up clompy things on their feet.*

The human was sitting on a round object, reaching into a plastic bag next to him and pulling out nuts and seeds. One by one, he popped them into his mouth, chewed up a storm, then spit the shells out onto the road. Suddenly, while the human was chewing, the bag of nuts and seeds

disappeared as if it had never been there. Flitter swooped down to investigate and saw the tip of a black tail sticking out from under the red dragon.

"Snout!" she called. "Give that human back his food."

"Come on," Snout said with a crooked little grin. "I'm just borrowing it. I'm planning to give him back all the empty shells."

When the human reached down to grab another handful of seeds and nuts, he realized the bag was gone. He jumped to his feet and looked from side to side. Nothing. He got on his knees and looked under the red dragon.

Not wanting to get caught, Snout hurried away, holding the bag in his teeth.

"Hey, weasel!" the human yelled. "Bring me back that bag! That's my power snack. I need energy if I'm going to change this flat tire."

The human ran down the dusty road after Snout. Flitter swooped low to get a better look at the round object he'd been sitting on. It looked just like the spaceship in the pond! And there were more under the red dragon!

Oh no! she thought. *Sal was right. There are lots of aliens ready to attack us.*

Flitter knew she had to tell her friends right away. She zoomed back to the pond.

"Bad news," she panted as she landed on a blade of grass. "There are three more spaceships up on the road, and they look really dangerous."

"We're doomed!" Sal cried.

"That's not even the worst part," Flitter said. "The spaceships are right there next to a red metal dragon!"

"Not a dragon!" Harry moaned. "Walter the big-mouth bass told me dragons love to eat fish.

I bet it's going to roast me with its flaming breath and have me for dinner."

"Calm down, Harry, and let me go over the clues," Willow said. She tapped her webbed foot like she always did when she was thinking hard.

"Did the dragon breathe fire?" she asked Flitter. "No."

"Did it have pointy claws?"

"No."

"Did it have huge wings?"

"No. It just had a big, flat back with four doors with shiny handles and some chairs inside."

"Hmm, wait just a minute," Willow said, tapping her foot some more. "I don't think you saw a dragon. I think it was a truck. I've seen humans rolling around in them at the campsite."

"Human trucks roll around on alien spaceships?" Flitter asked.

"They're called tires!" Sal said. "I remember now! I was nearly squished by one last summer when I was hanging out listening to their campfire ghost stories. I got so scared, I could barely move when I saw the truck coming. I got out in time, but I'm sure I left a puddle behind."

"That's more than I wanted to know," Harry moaned.

"Guys," Willow said, "knock it off and let me think like a detective. So a human is on the road. He is putting a new tire on his truck. That means he must have taken off the old one. I bet he rolled it down the hill and that's how it landed in our pond! Poof! Detective Duck solves the case!"

"Willow, you're a genius! See, I told you that you can be just as great as Detective Detect-O," Sal said.

"Not so fast." Harry sighed, letting out a cloud of stinky breath. "Willow may have solved one mystery, but this isn't over. How do we get the tire out of the pond? I do not want to be sucking up bits of rubber for the rest of my life."

"Well, we can't carry it," Flitter said. "I can only lift a mosquito, maybe an ant, but anything heavier and I crumble like a dirt clump. The rest of you aren't much stronger."

"How about we find a superhero to zap it away with his electric fingers?" Sal suggested. "Like they did in *Finger Man Meets the Evil Toe*."

"Do you know any superheroes?" Willow asked.

"Only on paper," Sal answered. "But you're smart, Willow. I'm sure you'll figure out how to get that evil tire out of our pond."

"I'll try," Willow said. "But I'm still just a little duck."

"Even a little duck can make a big difference," Sal said.

Sal was right. Willow knew that this was her chance to be a real detective. That rubber tire was polluting her beautiful home. It was up to her to find a way to get rid of it. But how?

She opened her Stuff Box and looked through her collection. There was a piece of rope. A little blue whistle. The metal spoon. An extra-bouncy pink rubber ball. One smooth, pointy rock. Two pine cones. And of course, lots of twigs and colorful leaves.

There must be something in here that can help me save the pond, she thought.

She took out all the objects and laid them on the ground in front of her.

"Think," she said to herself. "Think hard. Like a detective."

Sadly, not one idea popped into her duck brain. Maybe her Stuff Box didn't have the answers.

Then suddenly, she heard someone splashing in the shallow water. It was Tad the tadpole.

"Willow, we need help," he peeped. "A big black thing is floating toward my mom's restaurant. It's going to crush it if we don't do something fast."

Tad's mom, a lovely green frog name Franny, ran a small café on a lily pad in the center of the pond. The pond creatures often stopped by for a lunch of flies with a side of moss.

"That big black thing is called a tire," Willow explained to Tad.

"Whatever it is, we have to get it out before it sinks our whole lily pad." Tad let loose a flood of wet tadpole tears.

"Don't worry," Willow said. "Go tell your mother I'm on the case."

Tad swam away as fast as his tail could push him, which wasn't all that fast. Tadpole tails are very short.

Willow stared up at the sky, hoping she would see an idea floating by. She didn't. All she saw was Aaron the heron coming in for a landing.

Aaron the heron! Yes, he could help! A plan took shape in her mind.

"Poof!" she said. "Detective Duck is on the case."

CHAPTER 4

"Aaron," Willow called before he had even completed his landing. "We need your help! Really! Truly! Seriously! Right now!"

Aaron stretched his long white neck and stood on one leg, as herons do.

"Slow down, ducky," he said. "I've just flown in, and boy, are my wings tired!"

"You can rest later," Willow said. "We need your wing power now. We don't have a minute to waste."

She reached into her Stuff Box and pulled out the long piece of rope. She tied one end around Aaron's feathery body. He giggled.

"This is no laughing matter," Willow said.

"I can't help it if I'm ticklish," he said.

"Being ticklish is all in your mind," Willow told him.

"No, it isn't," Aaron answered. "It's under my wings."

"Aaron, we don't have time for this," Willow said. "Come with me."

She jumped into the water and headed to the center of the pond. Aaron followed behind her. When they reached the tire, Willow saw that it had already crushed many of the lily pads. It was dangerously close to Franny's Café. Poor Franny looked so frightened. All she could do was cuddle little Tad and kiss him with her long froggy tongue.

"We're here," Willow called out. "We'll save you." Then, turning to Aaron, she said, "Step onto the tire."

He climbed up the side and perched on top of the tire with his long, skinny legs.

Willow took the loose end of the rope into her bill and dove underwater through the center of the tire. She wrapped the rope around the tire and tied it in a double knot.

"Now all you have to do," she said to Aaron, "is fly to the road and drag this back to the red truck."

Aaron flapped his wings as hard as he could and tried to take off, but the tire barely moved.

"You need to flap faster, Aaron!" Willow cried.

"I'm trying!" he said. "But I can't get up in the air. The tire is too heavy. I'm a heron, not a forklift."

"Hmm," Willow said. "Here's another problem for Detective Duck to solve."

Willow swam back to the bank where Sal and Flitter and Harry were waiting for her.

"Aaron can't lift the tire," she told them.

"I can help push it," Harry said. "I'm an old fish, but I still have some sail in my tail."

"I can't swim, but I can fly above you and tell you which way to go," Flitter said.

"And I can cheer you guys on from the shore," Sal said. "Two, four, six, eight, who do we appreciate? The Pond Squad! The Pond Squad! Yaaaay!"

"Cheering is good, but it doesn't move tires," Willow said.

All the noise had attracted Snout, who stuck his head out of a clump of nearby ferns.

"What's going on?" he asked. "If there's food involved, I want in."

"You're not welcome here," Willow said. "We're on an important mission to save our pond, and you don't give a squirrel's tooth about our environment. Now go!"

"Make me!" he snarled.

Willow reached into her Stuff Box, pulled out the pink bouncy ball, and balanced it on her webbed foot. With a mighty flip of her foot, she sent the ball sailing through the air. She had great aim, and the ball landed smack on Snout's nose.

Bonk!

"Ow!" he yelped, tucking his long black tail between his legs and running off into the bushes.

Like most bullies, Snout ran away when things got tough.

Willow shuffled everything around in her Stuff Box until she found the little blue whistle. She blew three short blasts, her special signal to call her father. A few minutes passed, but he didn't

appear. Just when she was starting to worry, Beaver McBeaver popped his head out of the water.

"You called, my darling duckling?" he said, pulling a blackberry vine from between his two front teeth.

"What took so long, Dad?"

"I caught that Snout jumping into our supply of roots and vines, which I was going to use for our salad tonight," Willow's father explained. "But don't worry. I scared him away with a smack of my tail."

"Like father, like daughter," Sal laughed.

"Speaking of tails," Willow said, "Dad, I need to borrow yours."

"Sorry, dear, it doesn't come off."

"I know that! I need your powerful tail to help us push a big tire out of our pond."

"Oh no," he said. "Not another tire! Years ago, before you were born, one of those smashed into my dam and almost destroyed it."

"Don't those humans care about how their trash harms our beautiful wilderness?" Harry grumbled.

"Not to mention my living room," Beaver said.

"Well, I have a plan to get rid of that tire forever," Willow said. "It's called Operation Push and Pull. Are you in, Dad?"

"I'm in!" He held up his front paw. "Give me five."

"You know I don't have five toes like you," Willow said, holding up her foot. "All I have is a web."

"That will do."

The father and daughter high-fived in their own special way, just like they had been doing for years.

From across the pond, Franny let out a loud croak. Willow whipped around and saw the tire crashing onto her lily pad café.

"Hurry, Willow!" Aaron called. "My legs are wobbling. I can't hang on much longer."

"Here we go, everyone," Willow said, jumping into the water. "Operation Push and Pull starts now!"

CHAPTER 5

Sal jumped on Willow's back and the Pond Squad swam to the tire as fast as they could.

"It's about time you got here," Aaron said. "My knees are getting all wrinkled from standing in the water for so long."

"Listen up, everyone," Willow said. "Here's the plan. Aaron, you take off and pull the tire toward the shore. Dad, Harry, and I will push from behind."

"Let me take a few deep breaths to get my strength up," Harry said.

"Just keep your lips closed," Sal told him. "No offense, but your fishy breath clogs up my nose."

"My friend Tessie the trout thinks my breath smells heavenly."

"Sounds like her nose is clogged up too."

"Okay, listen," Willow called out. "There's no time for chatter. Everyone, do your job. On the count of three. One. Two. Three!"

Aaron spread his huge wings and took off. The rope tightened and the tire started to move. Harry, Beaver, and Willow pushed from behind with all their might.

"Go, team, go!" Sal cheered.

As the tire moved, it filled with water and grew very heavy.

"Aaron, flap harder!" Willow shouted.

"I'm trying," he answered. "But I'm pretty flapped out."

"We'll never make it to the shore," Sal said.

Willow's mind was in full detective mode, and another solution popped into her head. She swam to the front of the tire and pulled the red ribbon from her ponytail. She attached it to the rope, picked up the loose end with her bill, and then started to pull too.

"Oh, that's better," Aaron said. "Now it's easier to move this ridiculous thing."

Working together, the Pond Squad slowly pushed and pulled the tire toward the shore. Flitter flew above them, shouting directions.

"More to the left, guys!" she said. "Watch out for the log. It's covered in seagull poop. Good, getting close! Don't give up now."

The encouragement gave Aaron a new burst of strength. His powerful wings flapped hard and pulled the tire like a tugboat. At last, the exhausted team reached the shore.

"We did it!" they shouted.

There was high-fiving, high-webbing, high-winging, and high-tailing all around.

"Good work, team!" Willow said. "But we still have to finish the job. We need to get this ugly rubber tire away from our pond."

"Beaver McBeaver is still on duty," her dad said. "I'd go to the ends of the earth for you, my darling duckling."

Willow reached into her Stuff Box and grabbed the pointy rock. With Sal on her back and Flitter leading the way, she led the rest of the team up the hill. Aaron helped from above and her dad pushed from behind. Soon, they had dragged the heavy tire all the way up to the dirt road. The human was kneeling by the other tire, wiping sweat off his forehead with his hairy arm.

"Now we have to get that human to get rid of this thing," Sal said.

"Detective Duck has a plan," Willow said. "Sal,

can you help me write a word? I know all the letters you taught me. I just don't know the right order."

"Sure!" Sal said. He was very proud of his ability to read. "I can spell anything. Even 'shazam'!"

"Hang on to my back," Willow said. "And don't be scared. We're going face-to-face with him."

Willow took the rock in her bill and waddled across the road to where the human was kneeling. She let out a loud honk to get the human's attention.

"Hey, little ducky," the man said, turning to look at her. "What are you doing here?"

Oh, just wait and see, Willow thought. Then she turned to Sal and whispered, "Here's the word I need you to spell for me."

Sal told her each letter in order, and she used the rock to scratch the letters into the dirt road.

When she was finished, she'd spelled out R-E-C-Y-C-L-E.

The human's eyes nearly popped out of his head. He rubbed them twice and then looked again.

"I don't believe what I'm seeing," he said. "A duck who can write?!"

Willow flapped her wings to make herself look as big as possible. Staring directly at the man with her green-and-yellow eyes, she let out another loud honk.

"Okay, okay, I hear you," the man said. "You're right. I'll take this to the recycling center. You don't have to yell about it."

As the human loaded the tire onto the back of his truck, the Pond Squad could hear him talking to himself.

"I never dreamed I'd learn a lesson from a duck," he muttered. "What's next? Learning to shoot hoops from an elephant?"

"He sure is going to have some story to tell his human pals," Aaron said as they watched him drive away.

"See, Willow? That guy's going to tell the world about you," Sal said. "I told you you're going to be famous, just like Detective Detect-O!"

"Well, this famous duck detective is hungry," Willow said.

"I know just the place for lunch," her father said. "Franny's Café. Flies and moss for everyone. My treat!"

"Race you to the pond!" Willow said.

And then they all took off to celebrate at their beautiful, peaceful, tire-free pond.

ACKNOWLEDGMENTS

We are so appreciative of the work of the entire team at Abrams Kids for helping Detective Duck and her friends at the pond come to life.

To our publisher, Andrew Smith, our editor, Maggie Lehrman, and the ace marketing team of Hallie Patterson, Mary Marolla, and Jenny Choy, all our thanks for your efforts.

How lucky we are that Dan Santat agreed to illustrate this book. His massive talent, sense of humor, and joyful spirit are evident on every page. Dan, we are in awe of you!

Our agents, Esther Newberg and Ellen Goldsmith-Vein, have always supported our creative goals. We appreciate how much they have made our twenty-year writing collaboration possible. We are so proud of the body of children's books we have created together over all these years.

And finally, to the legions of environmental activists who put their hearts and minds into preserving our planet, we are grateful for your dedication and commitment. Detective Duck joins us in the hope that all our ponds and waterways will thrive and be protected for the natural wonders they are.

—Henry Winkler and Lin Oliver

ABOUT THE AUTHORS

Henry Winkler is an Emmy Award–winning actor, writer, director, and producer who has created some of the most iconic TV roles, including Arthur "the Fonz" Fonzarelli on *Happy Days* and Gene Cousineau on *Barry*.

Lin Oliver is a children's book writer and a writer and producer for both TV and film. She is the cofounder of the Society for Children's Book Writers and Illustrators (SCBWI) and is the managing director of the SCBWI Impact and Legacy Fund.

ABOUT THE ILLUSTRATOR

Dan Santat is the *New York Times* bestselling author of over one hundred books for children, including *Are We There Yet?*, *After The Fall*, and *The Adventures of Beekle: The Unimaginary Friend*, for which he won the Caldecott Medal. He lives in Southern California with his wife, two kids, and many, many pets.

STAY TUNED FOR THE NEXT

DETECTIVE
DUCK
MYSTERY!